For Sarah, my twin sister

First published in the United Kingdom in 2002 by
The Chicken House, 2 Palmer Street, Frome, Somerset, BA11 1DS
This edition published in 2003

Printed and bound in Singapore

British Library Cataloguing in Publication Data available

ISBN: 1 903434 63 7

# Do Your Ears Hang Low?

Illustrated by Caroline Jayne Church

The Chicken House

Do your ears hang low?

Do they wobble to and fro?

Can you tie them in a knot?

Can you tie them in a bow?

Can you throw them over your shoulder

Do your ears hang low?

Do your ears hang high?

Do they reach up to the sky?

Do they crinkle when they're wet?

Do they straighten when they're dry?

Can you wave
them at your
neighbour

with the minimum of labour?

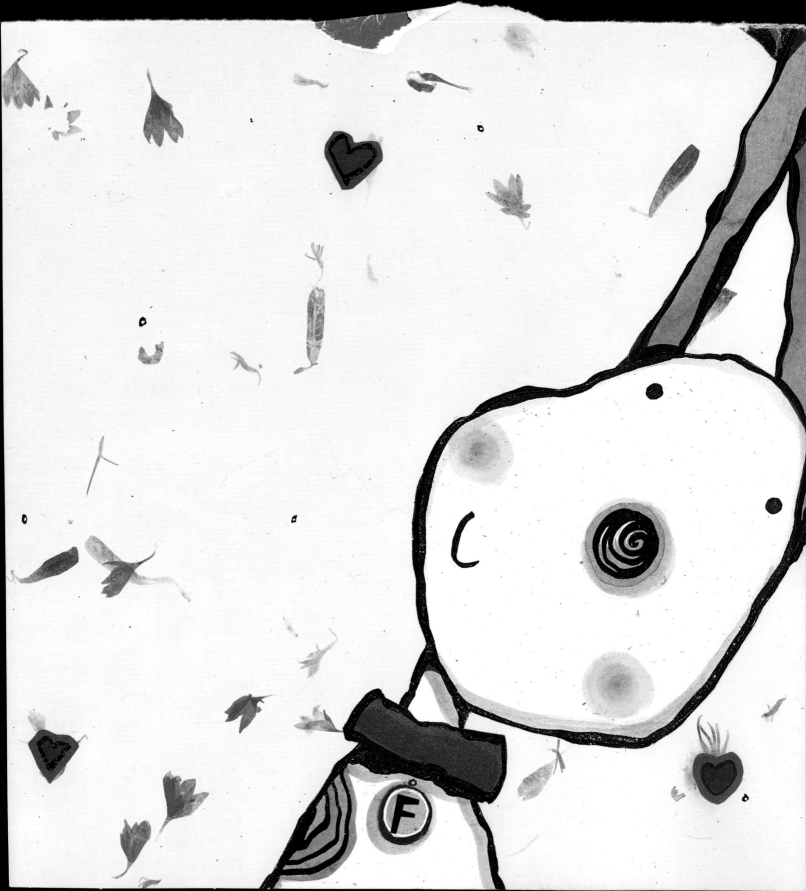

# Do Your Ears Hang Low ACTIONS!

**1** Do your ears hang low?

**2**  Do they wobble to and fro?

**3**  Can you tie them in a knot?

**4**  Can you tie them in a bow?

**5** Can you throw them over your shoulder like a regimental soldier?

**6** Do your ears hang low?

**7**  Do your ears hang high?

**10** Do they straighten when they're dry?

**8**  Do they wave up in the sky?

**11**  Can you wave them at your neighbour with the minimum of labour?

**9**  Do they crinkle when they're wet?

**12** Do your ears hang high!